T1-BLH-350

SKELLY
& FEMUR

SIMON & SCHUSTER BOOKS FOR YOUNG READERS

An imprint of Simon & Schuster Children's Publishing Division

1230 Avenue of the Americas, New York, New York 10020

Copyright © 2009 by Jimmy Pickering

SIMON & SCHUSTER BOOKS FOR YOUNG READERS is a trademark of Simon & Schuster, Inc.

Book design by Laurent Linn

The text for this book is set in Stanyan.

The art for this book was created by using mixed media.

Manufactured in China

10 9 8 7 6 5 4 3 2 1

Library of Congress Cataloging-in-Publication Data

Pickering, Jimmy.

Skelly & Femur / Jimmy Pickering.—1st ed.

p.   cm.

Summary: Skelly the skeleton girl and her dog, Femur, search for
the many things that have suddenly gone missing in Skelly Manor.

ISBN: 978-1-4169-7143-6 (hardcover)

[1. Skeleton—Fiction. 2. Bones—Fiction. 3. Dogs—Fiction.

4. Lost and found possessions—Fiction.] I. Title.

PZ7.P55252Sj 2009

[E]—dc22

2008006704

To Corey Albert. Thank you for bringing life back to this SKELETON BOY!

Thank you, Mom and Dad.

SKELLY
& FEMUR

Written and illustrated by
JIMMY PICKERING

SIMON & SCHUSTER BOOKS FOR YOUNG READERS
New York   London   Toronto   Sydney

My name is

SKELLY,

and this is my dog,

FEMUR.

We live in this
HOUSE,
high on a hill.

My DRESS was missing its BUTTONS.

Femur's DOG BONE was missing too

"It's uncivilized! Our SPOONS are missing!"

"My UMBRELLA is missing. Now I must stay indoors."

"Honey, our DISHES
have vanished."
"We've nowhere to
put our cake."

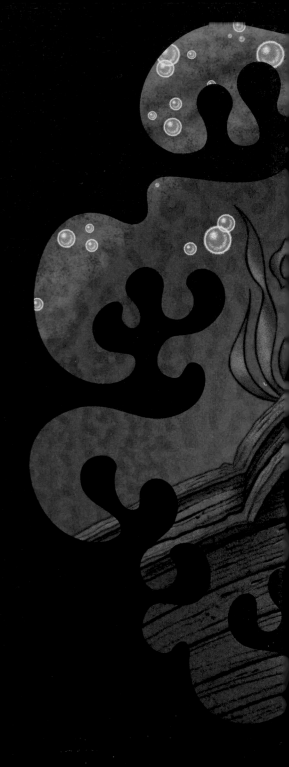

"My rusty ANCHOR is not here."

We were stumped.

That's when we heard it . . .

a STRANGE NOISE

from up in the attic.

Quietly we walked up the stairs.

I peeked through
the keyhole,

then opened
the door.